the CRitteR club

Amy and the Emerald Snake

by Callie Barkley 💜 illustrated by Tracy Bishop

LITTLE SIMON

New York London Toronto Sydney New Delhi

This book is a work of fiction. Any references to historical events, real people, or real places are used fictitiously. Other names, characters, places, and events are products of the author's imagination, and any resemblance to actual events or places or persons, living or dead, is entirely coincidental.

 LITTLE SIMON

An imprint of Simon & Schuster Children's Publishing Division · 1230 Avenue of the Americas, New York, New York 10020 · First Little Simon paperback edition December 2022. Copyright © 2022 by Simon & Schuster, Inc. All rights reserved, including the right of reproduction in whole or in part in any form.

LITTLE SIMON is a registered trademark of Simon & Schuster, Inc., and associated colophon is a trademark of Simon & Schuster, Inc. For information about special discounts for bulk purchases, please contact Simon & Schuster Special Sales at 1-866-506-1949 or business@simonandschuster.com.

The Simon & Schuster Speakers Bureau can bring authors to your live event. For more information or to book an event contact the Simon & Schuster Speakers Bureau at 1-866-248-3049 or visit our website at www.simonspeakers.com.

Designed by Brittany Fetcho.

The text of this book was set in ITC Stone Informal Std.

Manufactured in the United States of America 1022 LAK 10 9 8 7 6 5 4 3 2 1

Cataloging-in-Publication Data for this title is available from the Library of Congress.

ISBN 978-1-6659-2827-4 (hc)

ISBN 978-1-6659-2826-7 (pbk)

ISBN 978-1-6659-2828-1 (ebook)

Table of Contents

chapter 1

A Weekend Guest

From the waiting room, Amy Purvis heard her mom ending a phone call in the vet clinic office. Dr. Purvis was a veterinarian. Amy figured she was talking to a new pet owner. Maybe someone whose cat needed their shots. Or someone whose dog had eaten chocolate. Her mom got a lot of those calls.

"Mom!" Amy called. "I'll be in the car!"

Amy didn't want to be late to meet her friends at The Critter Club. That was the animal rescue shelter Amy had started with her best friends, Ellie, Liz, and Marion.

"Okay!" Amy's mom called back.
"I'm right behind you!"

They hopped into the minivan.

"That was your dad on the phone," Amy's mom said.

"Oh!" Amy replied in surprise. So, not a pet owner after all. Amy's dad and mom were divorced. He lived in Orange Blossom, just one town over.

"Chloe is going to come stay for the weekend," Dr. Purvis continued. "How does that sound?"

"Really?" Amy cried out in delight. "That sounds amazing!" Amy's dad had remarried a woman named Julia. And Chloe was Julia's daughter. But Chloe was *nothing* like the evil stepsisters in fairy tales.

Amy was so excited!

"And that's not all," Dr. Purvis said. "There's a gems and minerals exhibit at the Natural History Museum. I thought we could take Chloe."

Amy thought that was the best idea. "Chloe will *love* that," she said. Chloe was very into gems. She and her friends had started a jewelry-making club. They called it the Sapphire Society.

Now Amy was even more excited to get to The Critter Club. She wanted to tell her friends about Chloe's visit!

Dr. Purvis pulled up to a barn. It belonged to their friend Ms. Sullivan. A while back, Amy and her friends had found Ms. Sullivan's lost puppy, Rufus. Then Ms. Sullivan had offered the big, empty barn for the girls to use for The Critter Club.

Inside, Amy found Liz and Marion. "I have news!" Amy told them excitedly. She looked around. "But where's Ellie?"

Just then, Ellie hurried in, out of breath. She was holding a small glass tank covered with a cloth.

For a moment, Amy forgot about Chloe.

"What's that?" Amy asked Ellie.

"A surprise!" Ellie replied with a smile. She put the tank down on a table. She paused dramatically with her hand on the cloth. Then she whisked it off.

Amy, Liz, and Marion all gasped.
Inside the tank was a snake! A
few stripes ran lengthwise down its
long, narrow body.

"Everyone," said Ellie, "meet
Noodle!"

Another Guest

Liz was still staring at the snake. "Is it yours?" she asked Ellie.

Ellie shook her head no. "Noodle belongs to my cousin Hailey," Ellie explained. "She and my aunt and uncle are on vacation. So Hailey asked if we could take care of him for a few days."

Ellie looked at her friends, waiting

for their response.

"I hope it's okay that I said yes," she added. "I should have asked you all first."

"Of course it's okay," Amy said.

Marion snapped into organization mode. "We'll need to do some research," she said. "We've never taken care of a snake."

"Wait!" Ellie cried. She pulled a folded paper out of her pocket. "Hailey left a bunch of instructions. 'Noodle likes frogs, worms, fish, and other bugs,'" she read from the paper. "He's definitely not a vegetarian!"

All the girls looked at Liz. She and her family were vegan. But Liz smiled. "Noodle is just part of the food chain," she said. "I get it."

For several minutes, the girls watched Noodle in awe. The way he slithered around was so different from other animals.

"I feel like I've seen a snake like Noodle before," Marion commented. She reached for her backpack on a nearby chair. Marion pulled out a science book. "We *are* doing that science unit on reptiles."

GARTER SNAKE

Marion flipped through the pages. She stopped at a photo in the reptile chapter.

Amy read the caption. "A garter snake! I've heard of them. It says here they're a common snake in the wild." She looked up at her friends. "And not venomous. So that's good news for us!"

They all sighed with relief and laughed.

"I've definitely seen one in our yard," Liz declared.

Marion nudged Amy. "Hey," she said, "when you came in you said you had news."

"Right!" Amy cried. She'd been so distracted by Noodle. But now Amy told them. "My stepsister Chloe is coming this weekend."

"Oh, wow!" said Liz. "That's so fun!"

"Can you bring her here," Marion asked, "so we can meet her at last?"

It was funny to think that her friends hadn't met Chloe. Amy had told them a lot about her. Chloe was an only child, like Amy. They both loved Nancy Drew mysteries. Chloe loved gems and sparkly dresses. And the Sapphire Society was Chloe and her three best friends. It sort of sounded like The Critter Club!

"Yes!" Ellie said. "I want to meet Chloe too."

Amy laughed and nodded. She told her friends about the gem exhibit. "We're going to take her to the museum," she said. "But there will be time for her to meet you, too." Amy beamed. "I really think you're going to love her!"

Chapter 3

Sweet Reunion

On Friday after school, Amy waited in the loop outside Santa Vista Elementary. Her mom was coming to pick her up.

And Chloe would be with her!

Amy clapped as she spotted the minivan. It was ten cars back in the pickup lane. Slowly, the line inched forward. Amy could see a girl with shiny dark hair in braids looking out an open window.

"Amy!" Chloe called. She waved frantically.

Amy waved back. Finally, the van reached the load-in area. The back door slid open. Chloe hopped out.

"Chloe!" Amy cried. "I'm so glad you're here!"

They hugged each other tightly.

Then Amy pulled back. She looked down at Chloe's dress. It was blue and covered in sparkles. "I love your dress!" Amy said. "Is it new?"

Chloe nodded. "Look!" she said. "It even has pockets!"

Amy laughed. "My friend Ellie has a red one kind of like that," she said.

Amy climbed into the back seat. Chloe sat next to her.

"Mom," Amy said, "could we maybe stop at Scoops to celebrate Chloe being here?"

Scoops was the best ice cream place in town.

Dr. Purvis looked at the time on the dashboard. "Sure!" she said. "But I thought you wanted to take Chloe to The Critter Club meeting?"

"I do," Amy replied. "But we have time before it starts."

So they headed toward downtown Santa Vista. Amy and Chloe chatted nonstop on the way. Chloe told Amy about the school play she was in. Amy told Chloe about the mystery she was reading.

At Scoops, they mulled over the menu of ice cream flavors. Chloe couldn't decide between mint chip and almond fudge. Amy suggested they get both. "We can split them!" she said.

Then they sat down at an outdoor table.

"I'm so excited for you to meet my friends," Amy said to Chloe.

Chloe nodded and looked down at her spoon. She bit her lip. All of a sudden, Chloe looked worried. "Do you think they'll . . . like me?" Chloe asked softly.

Amy was so surprised by the question that she was speechless for a moment. A memory came flashing back. It was when she and Chloe had first met. Chloe had acted strangely at first—even a bit mean, or so Amy thought. But it turned out Chloe had just been nervous and worried that Amy didn't like her.

Now it seemed Chloe was having the same worries— but about Amy's friends.

"They were so excited when I told them you were coming!" Amy said to Chloe.

When they were done with their ice cream, Amy linked her arm through Chloe's.

"I just know they'll like you,"
Amy assured her. "Come on. You'll
see."

A Warm Welcome

Ellie, Marion, and Liz were standing in a row outside The Critter Club. *That's nice of them*, thought Amy as they pulled up in the minivan. She hoped it would make Chloe feel special. "They're waiting to welcome you!" Amy said.

Chloe cracked a smile. "They do look excited."

Amy laughed. Ellie was practically jumping up and down.

They got out of the car and Amy led Chloe over. "Everyone, meet Chloe!" she said. Amy introduced her friends one by one.

"Hi, Chloe!" Ellie cried. "I really love your dress."

Chloe smiled. "Amy said you might. Nice to meet you!"

Marion gave a little wave. "We could not wait for you to get here," she said. "What took you guys so long?"

Amy told them about stopping for ice cream. "Sorry," she said. "My fault."

Then Liz complimented Chloe's bracelet. Chloe thanked her and said she'd made it. That reminded Liz. "We want to hear all about the Sapphire Society!" she said.

"Okay!" Chloe replied.

Before Amy knew what was happening, her friends turned and led Chloe into the barn.

Wow! Amy thought. *That went well!* She hurried to catch up so that she could show Chloe around The Critter Club.

As Amy stepped inside, Ellie was already showing Chloe the snake tank.

Amy gasped. *Noodle!*

Oh, why hadn't Amy remem-
bered before now? Chloe was afraid
of animals. Amy knew this from
their first meeting. A dog in the
park had run after Chloe, barking.
The dog just wanted to play. But
Chloe had been frightened.

If Chloe was afraid of a dog, what would she think of a snake?

"He's my cousin's garter snake," Ellie was saying. "His name is Noodle."

Amy held her breath, bracing for Chloe's reaction.

"Wow," Chloe said quietly, almost in awe. "He's super cool."

Huh?

Amy couldn't believe it! Chloe didn't seem scared at all. In fact, Chloe was putting her face right up to the glass wall. She was trying to get a closer look!

Amy hung back and sighed with relief.

Marion started telling Chloe all about the other animals they'd taken care of at The Critter Club: dogs, cats, pigs, turtles, frogs, chickens . . .

Chloe seemed impressed. Then Ellie and Chloe chatted for a while about fashion. Chloe showed Ellie the cool pockets on her dress. "Yes!" Ellie exclaimed. "Why don't more dresses have them? Even fancy dresses need pockets."

Chloe agreed.

Later, Liz and Chloe discovered that they both loved drawing. Chloe told Liz that she sketched out her jewelry designs before making anything. Liz pulled out her own sketchbook. Chloe flipped through it as Liz looked on.

Off to the side, Amy started to feel a little bit left out. But she pushed the feeling away.

I should just be happy that everyone is getting along so well, Amy told herself.

And she was.

But Amy was also glad when it was time for her and Chloe to head home. Now they could have some sister-bonding time!

Pajamas and Making Plans

Later, at Amy's house, she and Chloe got ready for bed. Amy's mom had pulled out the air mattress. Chloe rolled out her sleeping bag on it.

Amy often had sleepovers on Friday nights. She, Marion, Ellie, and Liz took turns hosting. But it was kind of nice to have just one guest, Amy thought.

"So what do you want to do?" Amy asked Chloe.

Chloe shrugged. "I don't know," she said. "Maybe tell me more about The Critter Club. I had so much fun there. Your friends are *so* great!"

Chloe listed her favorite parts of the day: Ellie's funny story about the pig they'd taken care of; Marion showing Chloe all their  chore charts and the very organized supply closet.

"And looking through Liz's sketchbook," Chloe added. "Her drawings are so good!"

Amy agreed. But her heart sank a little. Chloe hadn't mentioned anything about *her*.

Amy tried to change the subject. "I still don't know that much about the Sapphire Society," she said. "What are your friends like? When do you get together? What do you do with the jewelry you make?"

Chloe's eyes lit up. She immediately began telling Amy all about it. Chloe and her friends Sarah, Jake, and Anna had started the club in kindergarten.

"We liked looking around for shiny stones at recess," Chloe said. "Then we figured out we all had rock collections at home." Chloe laughed at the memory.

So the friends started having meetings. They'd all bring their rock collections. Sometimes they would trade. Most were rocks they had found outside. A few were special— like geodes or souvenir rocks you can buy in a gift shop.

"Then one day I started making jewelry," Chloe said. "I used some of my sparkly stones. I got some gem beads at craft stores. My friends wanted to do it too."

They kept some of the things they made. They gave some as gifts. They even sold a few at a craft fair once.

"That's when we came up with the name," Chloe said. "To put on our sign: the Sapphire Society!"

"It's catchy," Amy said.

"Thanks," Chloe replied. "Oh! That reminds me." She jumped up and went over to her bag. She dug through it until she found a big envelope.

Chloe emptied the contents onto her sleeping bag. There were pouches of stones, gems, and beads. And there were spools of embroidery thread in rainbow colors.

"I brought supplies for friendship bracelets," Chloe said. "Maybe we could make some tomorrow."

Amy beamed. "I would love to do that!" she exclaimed.

It was something they could do, just the two of them, when they got back from the museum.

The museum! They'd have their special trip to the museum together, too.

After lights out, Amy drifted off to sleep, thinking those happy thoughts.

Change of Plans

"Good morning, you two!" Dr. Purvis said. "And you're already dressed!" She was prying a waffle out of the waffle iron.

Amy and Chloe plopped down at the kitchen table.

"Yep!" Amy said. "We are ready! Can we go to the museum right after breakfast, Mom?"

Dr. Purvis smiled mischievously. "Yes," she said. "And . . . I have a surprise. I thought it might be fun to invite Marion, Ellie, and Liz, too."

Chloe gasped with excitement. Amy opened her mouth to object.

But Amy's mom went on. "So I called their parents. And they all can come!"

Chloe clapped. "Amazing!" She turned to Amy. "Right, Amy?"

Amy smiled but didn't say anything. She knew she should be excited too. But Amy had thought the museum would be . . . *their* thing.

Outside the museum entrance, they found Liz, Marion, Ellie, and their parents.

"I'm so glad you all came too!" Chloe told them. "This is going to be the best day."

Amy and her friends had been to the museum many times. Once, they'd even spent a night there! So their parents let them go through the gems and minerals exhibit mostly on their own.

"Stay together," Marion's dad said. "We'll be right over here."

"Let's meet back here in forty-five minutes," Dr. Purvis suggested.

The girls agreed. Then they set off excitedly.

The exhibit hall was dimly lit. It took a moment for Amy's eyes to adjust.

But when they did, the first thing she saw was an enormous purple geode in the middle of the room.

"Wow!" was all Amy could think to say.

Ellie laughed. "It's bigger than we are!"

The girls read the info card in front of the geode. "I thought so," said Chloe. "It's amethyst."

"Chloe," said Liz, "what does a sapphire look like?"

"I'll show you!" Chloe replied. "Let's find one."

Chloe led the way around the display cases. The bright overhead lights made all the gems glitter and sparkle.

She pointed out rubies and emeralds. She showed them opals and jade.

"Here!" Chloe cried. She pointed to a brilliant blue gemstone in one of the cases. "That's a sapphire."

Ellie nudged Chloe. "Blue and sparkly—like your dress yesterday."

Chloe laughed.

Amy's friends asked Chloe lots of questions. They seemed very impressed by her gem knowledge.

Marion wandered over to a case of jewelry shaped like snakes. She read the card next to a gold and ruby snake ring: "To the Romans, a continuous snake was a sign of everlasting love."

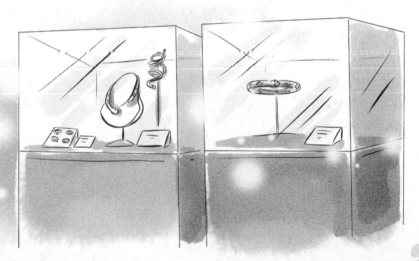

Liz read a card next to a silver snake armband: "The Greeks viewed snakes as symbols of wisdom."

Amy's eyes were locked on an emerald snake bracelet.

Next to Amy, Chloe noticed what she was looking at. "That one is my favorite too," Chloe whispered to Amy.

Amy smiled. "I love it," she replied. "Especially the line of gems running down it. It reminds me of—"

"Noodle!" Chloe and Amy said at the same time.

Amy's Blue Mood

The girls were nearing the end of the exhibit.

"I have an idea," Chloe said. She turned to face the others. "Amy and I were planning to make friendship bracelets later. I know how to make a snake one. I could teach you all if you want." Chloe shrugged.

Marion nodded enthusiastically.

Ellie twirled with glee. Liz gave a thumbs-up.

Amy smiled. But her heart sank. She couldn't help feeling a little hurt. It was another thing that they were going to do, just she and Chloe.

Not anymore.

But Amy didn't want to ruin the fun. Or be rude to her friends.

Back in the lobby, the girls looked around the museum gift shop.

Amy looked over the pencils and magnets and key rings by the checkout. But she was not in the mood for shopping.

After a little while, Amy decided to wait in the lobby. As she walked out, she heard Chloe and Ellie giggling at the book rack.

At least some *of us are having a good time*, Amy thought.

Amy sat on a bench with her mom. The other girls' parents chatted nearby.

One by one, her friends came out of the gift shop.

Liz was carrying a small shopping bag. She pulled out a little notebook and pencil she had bought. "On the way home, I want to sketch a few of the things we saw," she told Amy.

Amy nodded.

Ellie came out with a bigger bag. Inside was a poster tube. She showed them the gem poster she'd bought.

Marion came out with a bunch of postcards. Some featured gems from the exhibit they'd seen. Others had photos from the dinosaur exhibit.

Amy was mostly quiet. She watched as the friends passed around their purchases. A small part of her wished she had bought something too.

After a few minutes, Amy looked around. Where was Chloe? She was the only one who hadn't come out.

"Mom," Amy said, a little worried, "have you seen Chloe?"

Dr. Purvis shook her head. "Let's go check on her," she replied. Together they took a few steps toward the gift shop.

Just then, Chloe came rushing out.

She was carrying a bag too.

"You got something?" Amy asked Chloe.

"Mm hmm," Chloe replied. But she kept on walking. Unlike Ellie, Liz, and Marion, Chloe didn't really seem interested in showing Amy what she had chosen.

They all headed toward the parking lot. Amy trailed behind everyone else, feeling just about as blue as a sapphire.

Tied in Knots

The parents dropped the girls back at The Critter Club. They wanted to check on Noodle.

Liz didn't want to be the one to feed him. So Marion took care of it. She put some worms in Noodle's bowl.

"Noodle," Liz said, "did you know you were a symbol of wisdom in ancient times?"

"And love!" added Ellie.

Chloe was eyeing one of the tables in the barn. "This would be a good place to work on our snake bracelets," Chloe said.

"Let's do it!" Ellie exclaimed. Liz and Marion agreed.

"Sure," said Amy. "Why not?"

So Chloe got the supplies out of her bag. She said each of them should cut four different-colored strands of embroidery thread.

"And you'll need one bead," Chloe told them. "For the snake's head."

Then Chloe demonstrated how to get started. She taped her thread ends to the table. She held one color thread in one hand. She held all the other threads in the other hand. Then she started tying knots.

"Take one color thread," said Chloe. "Tie a forward knot around all the others. And then repeat. See?"

Chloe demonstrated. The girls watched carefully.

"Wait," said Ellie. "What's a for-ward knot?"

Marion frowned.

Amy was very confused too.

Liz was the only one who seemed to get it right away. Being as crafty as she was, Amy was sure Liz had made friendship bracelets before.

But Chloe was very patient. "It's okay," she said. "I'll show you a bunch of times. It can definitely be tricky at first."

So Chloe demonstrated again.

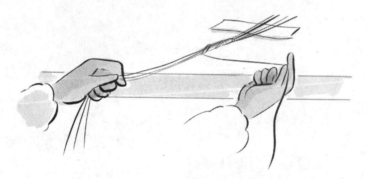

This time, Marion said, "Ah hah." She started knotting.

And after the fourth time, Ellie said, "Oh! Okay." She began to work.

Meanwhile, Liz was on a roll. "Look!" she said. "After a while, it starts to look like this." A line of knots spiraled around the outside of the bracelet. "Like a snake!"

But Amy still had no idea how to begin. "This thread over these?" she asked Chloe. "Or these over that one?"

Chloe moved her chair closer to Amy's. "It's okay," Chloe said. "The first time I made this, I had to restart it five times."

Chloe showed Amy the steps again, one at a time. She paused between each step so Amy could do it.

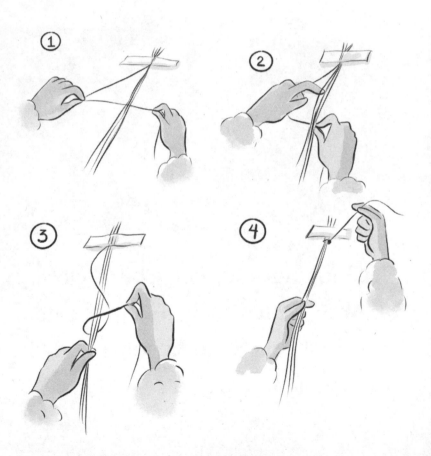

"Okay," Amy said. "I think I see." Each step wasn't hard. But when Amy tried to repeat them on her own, she felt lost again.

"I can't see it!" Amy cried out. She pushed her chair back and stood up. "What is a *forward knot*?!"

Amy was surprised at her own voice. She never really shouted.

All the girls were looking at her sympathetically. Amy's face flushed a bright red. Immediately, she felt awful.

She let go of the threads and ran out of the barn.

Chapter 9

Chloe's Surprise

Outside, Amy sat down on a low stone wall in Ms. Sullivan's yard. Almost right away, Ms. Sullivan's dog, Rufus, came bounding over. He put his head on Amy's knee.

Amy smiled. *Aw.* Rufus could tell she was sad. She patted Rufus's head. Already she felt a little bit better.

Then Chloe appeared at Amy's side. "What's the matter, Amy?" she asked.

Amy shook her head. "Nothing," she replied. "I don't know why I got so frustrated. I guess I'm just not very crafty."

Chloe nodded. She and Amy sat in silence for a few moments. Then Chloe said, "Are you sure there's nothing else? Something bothering you?"

Amy hesitated.

Chloe put her arm around Amy. "Come on," Chloe said. "You can tell me."

Amy looked Chloe in the eye. She knew Chloe really meant it.

So Amy took a deep breath and gathered the courage to say what was on her mind.

"I guess I've been feeling a little left out," Amy said. "You and my friends have been getting along . . . so well."

"Oh, Amy." Chloe gave her a big squeeze. "I had no idea you were feeling that way. I'm sorry. I *have* been trying hard to get along with Liz, Marion, and Ellie."

Amy nodded.

"But you know why?" Chloe went on. "It's because they're your friends. I know you care about them. And they care about you."

Chloe got up. "Wait here," she told Amy. "I want to show you something."

Chloe ran off. She came back holding a bag from the museum gift shop. Then she took out two small boxes. She handed one to Amy.

"Open it," Chloe said.

Amy took off the lid. Inside was a charm for a bracelet. It was in the shape of a snake.

And not just any snake. It was a replica of the emerald snake! The one that she and Chloe both loved! "For me?" Amy asked.

Chloe nodded. "And one for me."
Chloe took the lid off her box. She
had the exact same snake charm.

"I wanted to get something special," Chloe told her. "Just for the
two of us. I thought we could add it
to our snake bracelets."

*No wonder she didn't show me what
was in her bag,* Amy thought. *It was
a surprise for me!*

Amy wrapped her arms around Chloe and gave her a big hug. "I love it," Amy said. "I love it so much! Thank you, Chloe."

"You're welcome," Chloe replied. Amy's heart was full.

Friendship Circle

Amy and Chloe went back inside the barn. They sat down next to each other at the table. Slowly, step by step, Chloe showed Amy exactly how to make each knot.

Before long, Amy's snake bracelet was taking shape.

And Amy was getting the hang of it.

"You were right," Amy told Chloe. "It was tricky at first. But I understand now."

The girls talked and laughed as they tied knot after knot.

When Amy and Chloe were done, they got up and went to check on Noodle.

Amy noticed his water bowl was low. So she refilled it at the sink. Then they turned on Noodle's special heat and UV lamps. Hailey's instructions said he needed to be warm to digest his food.

Amy held her snake bracelet up to the glass. "What do you think, Noodle?" Amy asked him.

Liz, Marion, and Ellie came over too. Everyone's snake bracelet was a little bit different. Ellie had made hers with bright pink threads. Marion's had blues and purples. Liz had gone with pastels.

Amy's and Chloe's were both green to match their emerald snake charm. They each slid their charm onto their bracelet.

Then Chloe helped them all tie their bracelets onto their wrists. And Amy helped tie on Chloe's.

Standing in a circle, they all put their hands in the center. Amy admired the rainbow of colors.

She was happy they all had this souvenir. They could always remember their weekend with Chloe. And Noodle!

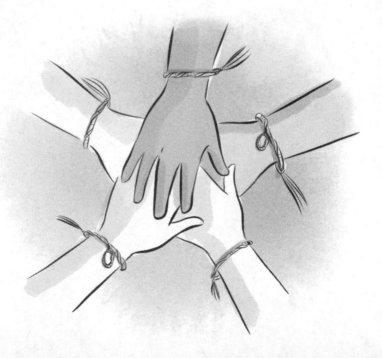

And she was happy that she and Chloe had something special for just the two of them, too.

the **CRiTTER** club

Join the club!